Grandpa Bodley
and the
Photographs

Grandpa Bodley
and the
Photographs

Caroline Castle *and* Peter Bowman

RED FOX

For
C.H.A.L.L.

A Red Fox Book

Published by Random House Children's Books
20 Vauxhall Bridge Road, London SW1V 2SA

A division of Random House UK Ltd
London Melbourne Sydney Auckland
Johannesburg and agencies throughout the world

3 5 7 9 10 8 6 4 2

First published in Great Britain by
Hutchinson Children's Books 1993

Red Fox edition 1994

Printed in Hong Kong

RANDOM HOUSE UK Limited Reg. No. 954009

ISBN 0 09 929011 1

One day Grandpa Bodley and Hutchinson were clearing out the
cupboard under the stairs when they came across a rusty old tin.
   'I wonder what's inside?' said Hutchinson.
   'Let's open it,' said Grandpa, 'then we'll find out.'

Grandpa held firmly on to the back of the tin while
Hutchinson pulled at the lid. It snapped open with a ping.
A ghostly bear loomed out at them from the dark box.
'Ahhhhh!' screeched Hutchinson, jumping back in fright.
'Silly,' laughed Grandpa. 'It's only a photograph.'

Hutchinson and Grandpa Bodley looked at the photograph.
The big teddy face seemed to be staring straight at them. Bodley
put on his glasses and studied it carefully. There was something
familiar about this strange bear. 'Yes, yes,' he said. 'Those ears,
that nose, that particular way of smiling . . . it's your Great-
granddad Dutton when he was a young bear. It's a self-portrait.'

Bodley turned the tin upside down. A great shower of photographs flew out and soon there were bears all over the floor. 'Do you know something,' said Grandpa in a whisper, 'I do believe we've found Great-granddad Dutton's famous photograph collection.'

With mounting excitement the two bears collected the photographs and carried them to the kitchen table.

'Well, what did I say,' said Grandpa Bodley, picking up the first one. 'Here he is again, on his wedding day.'

Hutchinson saw a very smart bear dressed in a funny long coat with a flower in the buttonhole. 'When was that?' he asked.

'Oh, years and years ago,' said Bodley. 'Before he got all crinkly and lost his fur.'

Hutchinson pulled another one from the middle of the pile. It
was of a small bear in a smart school uniform looking very prim
and stiff.

'Why, that's me!' exclaimed Grandpa Bodley, 'on my first day at big school. I was scared half to death. They were very strict in those days, so you had to watch out.'

'You don't look very comfortable,' said Hutchinson.

Grandpa laughed. 'I wasn't,' he said, rubbing his neck. 'I hated my school uniform. I can still feel that scratchy collar to this day.'

'Who's this teddy?' asked Hutchinson, picking up another photograph. It was a fuzzy snapshot of a pretty young bear reading a book.

'Oh, goodness me,' said Grandpa. 'It's Grandma Bodley when I first met her. I gave her that book for her birthday.'

'Where's Grandma Bodley now?' asked Hutchinson. 'Why isn't she here?'

Grandpa's eyes misted over. 'Ahem,' he said. 'There's a thing.' For a moment he looked very sad. Then he smiled and sniffed into his hanky. 'I think I've got a cold coming on,' he said.

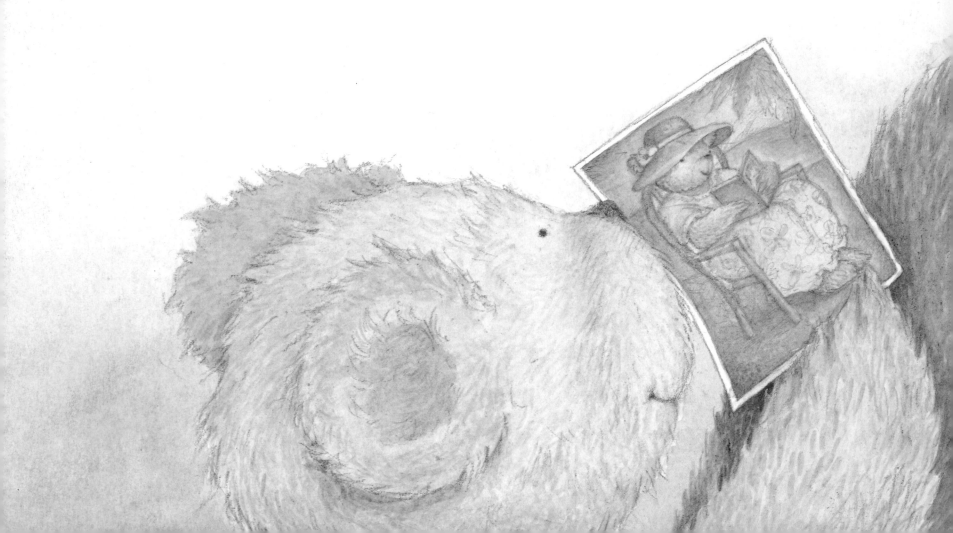

The next photograph was a bit blurry. Hutchinson held it up to the window. Grandpa took a deep breath. 'The coronation of Queen Elizabear the Second,' he said importantly. 'I drove the whole family to London in my new motorcar. We all dressed up for the occasion. Great-granddad was getting on a bit by then and needed a walking stick.'

It really was a beautiful picture, with the young queen waving to the crowd from a golden carriage. 'Hey,' said Hutchinson, 'she looks as if she's waving straight at Grandma Bodley.'

'I wouldn't be surprised if she was,' laughed Grandpa. 'Grandma fought her way to the front and nearly wore herself out cheering and waving.'

'Time we had a break,' said Grandpa.
'Why, it's nearly lunchtime.'
Grandpa Bodley made some tea and
Hutchinson helped with the sandwiches.

'Oh, happy memories,' sighed Grandpa, thinking fondly of Grandma Bodley.

Hutchinson gobbled down his sandwich as fast as he could. 'I'm ready for more photos now,' he said.

'Hold your horses,' laughed Grandpa. 'You can't rush a good cup of tea.'

After lunch Grandpa put his glasses back on and the two bears, the big old one and the very little young one, settled down to look at the rest of the photographs.

'Well I never,' said Grandpa. 'Here's our old house at Buttonear Road. And look, who do you think that is on the bicycle?'

Hutchinson looked hard. It was a small girl bear about four years old.

'I'll tell you who it is,' said Grandpa Bodley. 'It's your mum when she was a little bear. We bought her that bicycle for her birthday. She was very wobbly at first but she soon learned to ride. She was determined not to be afraid.'

Hutchinson loved the photograph. He had never thought of his mum as a little bear.

'Now here we are,' said Grandpa, picking up a photograph that had fallen on the floor. 'The great Oxford and Cambridge bear race. We took a picnic. There's your mum again and Grandma Bodley holding the flowers, and that's me with the glasses.'

'Look!' said Hutchinson, pointing to a small bear in a red jacket. 'He's taking the last piece of cake while no one's looking.'

'Aha,' said Bodley. 'It's my dreadful nephew Hamish. He was spoilt to death, and greedy with it. You know, I always wondered how that cake disappeared so quickly!'

Grandpa lay down on the sofa to stretch his legs.

'Look at this,' said Hutchinson. 'A Christmas one.'

Grandpa adjusted his glasses, peered closely, then laughed and laughed. It was Christmas time and the whole family was gathered round the tree. 'I remember this as if it were yesterday,' he said. 'There's Aunt Hamilton and my horrible nephew Hamish again. That photograph was taken just after he'd put a piece of holly on Great-grandma Dutton's chair as she was sitting down. If you look closely you'll see that he's crying.'

'What happened?' said Hutchinson.

'He got a smack, that's what,' said Grandpa. 'And about time too. He'd been so naughty, it's a wonder Father Christmas came at all.'

Hutchinson pounced on the next photograph with a shriek.

'I know who these are!' he cried. 'It's my mum and dad.'

'That's right,' said Bodley. 'It was taken just before their wedding. They were so much in love that they hardly noticed anyone else. Great-granddad Dutton was very old by then. Ninety-seven at least. He died the next year. Dear old thing.'

Hutchinson felt rather sad. 'But at least he left these photographs,' he said. 'To remember him by.'

They were nearing the end of the pile. Grandpa didn't say but Hutchinson could tell he was getting tired. He always rubbed his eyes when he felt sleepy.

They had come to the last photograph. Grandpa picked it up
carefully. It was of a very, very small bear all bristly and new and
wrapped up in a blue blanket.

'Who's that?' asked Hutchinson.

'Why, that's *you*, young teddy,' whispered Grandpa. 'Just after
you were born.' He walked over to his chair, leaned heavily back
and pulled Hutchinson onto his knee. Hutchinson touched the
old bear's cheek.

'Why are you crying, Grandpa?' he asked.

'Oh, I don't know,' sighed Grandpa. 'I must be getting old.'

And Hutchinson sat warm and tight on Grandpa's lap until the
sun went down and the old bear was asleep.